Be a Pirate

Diana Noonan
Photography by Lindsay Edwards

Contents

Be a Pirate

It is fun to be a pirate.

You can be a pirate, too!

A Pirate Captain

I am the captain of a pirate ship.

I put on an earring.

I put on
a pirate hat.

I put on a coat.

I put on a belt.

I am the captain.
I run the ship!

A Ship Hand

I am a ship hand
on the pirate ship.

I put a patch
on my eye.

I put a scarf
on my head.

I put on a vest.

I put on a belt.

I am a ship hand.
I help the captain!

Off We Go!

Off we go in our ship!